CANADA

Newfoundland and Labrador

Prince Edward Island

Quebec

Ontario

Nova Scotia

New Brunswick

ABC of Canada

For our parents, Bev and Brian, Peter and Christine — K.B. and P-H.G.

Kids Can Press acknowledges the financial support of the Government of Ontario, through the Ontario Media Development Corporation's Ontario Book Initiative; the Ontario Arts Council; the Canada Council for the Arts; and the Government of Canada, through the BPIDP, for our publishing activity.

Published in Canada by
Kids Can Press Ltd.
29 Birch Avenue
Toronto, ON M4V 1E2

Published in the U.S. by
Kids Can Press Ltd.
2250 Military Road
Tonawanda, NY 14150

www.kidscanpress.com

The artwork in this book was created in Adobe Illustrator.
The text is set in Providence-Sans Bold.

Edited by Jennifer Stokes and Debbie Rogosin
Designed by Per-Henrik Gürth and Julia Naimska
Printed in Hong Kong, China, by Wing King Tong Company Limited

The hardcover edition of this book is smyth sewn casebound.
The paperback edition of this book is limp sewn with a drawn-on cover.

CM 02 0 9 8 7 6 5 4
CM PA 04 0 9 8 7 6 5 4 3 2 1

National Library of Canada Cataloguing in Publication Data

Bellefontaine, Kim (Kim Anne)
ABC of Canada

ISBN 1-55337-340-5 (bound). ISBN 1-55337-685-4 (pbk.)

1. Alphabet — Juvenile literature. 2. Canada — Juvenile literature.
I. Gürth, Per-Henrik II. Title.

PE1155.B43 2002 j421'.1 C2001-901518-6

Kids Can Press is a Corus™ Entertainment company

ABC of Canada

illustrated by
Per-Henrik Gürth

written by
Kim Bellefontaine

Kids Can Press

A a
is for Arctic,
in the icy cold north.

B b
is for Beaver,
busy building a dam.

C c
is for Calgary Stampede —
days of rodeo fun. Yee haw!

D d
is for Dogsled,
gliding across the snow.

E e
is for Eagle,
soaring in the sky.

F f

is for Flag,
waving in a parade.

G g
is for Geese,
flying south
for the winter.

H h
is for Hockey —
he shoots, he scores!

I i

is for Ice Fishing,
on a frozen lake. Brrr!

J j

is for Jasper National Park, in the heart of the Rocky Mountains.

Kk
is for Kayak,
skimming across
the bay.

L l
is for Lobster,
snapping its
claws.

M m
is for Maple
Syrup — pour it
over pancakes.
Yum!

Nn
is for Niagara
Falls — hear
the water roar!

O o

is for Ottawa,
the capital
city of Canada.

P p
is for Peggy's Cove — its
lighthouse guides fishing
boats home.

Q q

is for Quebec City — take a carriage ride!

R r

is for Royal
Canadian Mounted
Police — see the
Mountie on
the horse.

S s
is for Salmon,
swimming upstream.

T t

is for Toronto, Canada's largest city.

U u
is for Underground,
where miners dig
deep for coal.

V v
is for Vancouver,
city by the ocean.

W w
is for Wheat,
growing in
prairie fields.

X x
is for X-Country Skiing,
through the snowy woods.

Y y
is for Yukon, where the
Northern Lights glow.

Z z

is for Zamboni,
cleaning the ice.